My Grandma's Guardian Angels

Two Girls and a Reading Corner

www.twogirlsandareadingcorner.com

MY GRANDMA'S GUARDIAN ANGELS

TWO GIRLS AND A READING CORNER

ISBN: 978-1-952879-11-1

Cover Art and Illustrations by DENNY POLIQUIT

Edited by MELANIE LOPATA

For permission requests, please email

twogirlsandareadingcorner@gmail.com

Place "Request for Permissions" in the subject line or contact:

Two Girls and a Reading Corner

PO Box 2404, Madison, AL 35758

To all who are reading this book:
there are angels all around us.
You can see them if you look hard enough.
Psalm 91:11 (NIV): "For he will command his angels concerning you to guard you in all your ways"

My grandma loved guardian angels,
I know this much is true.
She always believed,
That they are watching over you.

“They come in many forms,” she said.
“They don't always have wings to fly.
Some live amongst us here on Earth,
And never leave our side.”

She wore an angel pin on her sweater.
She collected angel notions big and small.
She even held an angel on her lap,
The greatest gift of all.

Peter
Rabbit

An angel can be a family member or a friend.
An angel can be anyone with a special place in your heart.
You know they will always be with you,
Even when you're far apart.

My grandma believed everyone has a guardian angel,
Not just from up above.
They are here to teach us kindness,
And to show us how to love.

God gave us guardian angels,
To help us to believe.
To show us His great love for us,
For which we humbly receive.

For everyone needs a special person,
To teach us and be with us until the very end.
My grandma is my guardian angel.
She's my forever friend.

Who is your guardian angel?
Do they live on Earth
or up in Heaven?
What lesson have they taught you?
This is an important question.

Who is your guardian angel?
(You can have more than one)
What makes them special to you?
What good things have you learned from them?
Describe your relationship.
Draw a picture of them here.

Acknowledgments

I dedicate this book to my very loving family and guardian angel [grandma], Beatrice Wood. I miss you a lot but am so glad to have you watch over me every day (say hi to Angel for me!) Till we meet again...xoxo

About the Author

Lindsay DeRollo is a children's book author and illustrator in Syracuse New York. She has written a ballet book series ("Sugarplum Stars"), a young adult short story ("Prima Ballerina") and a Christmas book ("A Christmas Kitten for Max"). She has always loved and felt drawn to guardian angels, which have a very special meaning for her.

About the Illustrator

Denny Poliquit is a children's book illustrator and a typography designer. She has an Associate's degree in computer technology, majoring in animation. She spends most of her time working and developing her skills and passion in designing. She always wants to share her knowledge and skills for the success for her authors and clients.

You can visit her site at dennyartportfolio.weebly.com.

This photograph is of my [late] grandma Beatrice Wood, whom this story is based upon. In it she is holding her cat named Angel.

Also, by Lindsay DeRollo:

"Sugarplum Stars" Series

Book 1 "Sugarplums and Shooting Stars"
Book 2 "Pinky Takes the Stage!"
Book 3 "If the Slipper Fits"

"A Christmas Kitten for Max"

" Prima Ballerina: A Short Story"

For more details and upcoming releases visit our website:
www.twogirlsandareadingcorner.com

Two Girls and a Reading Corner

P.O. Box 2404

Madison, AL 35758

www.ingramcontent.com/pod-product-compliance
Lightning Source LLC
LaVergne TN
LVHW070225110826
845147LV00003B/649

* 9 7 8 1 9 5 2 8 7 9 1 1 1 *